The 9/11 Terrorist Attacks

SEPTEMBER 11, 2001
THEN AND NOW

An imprint of Abdo Publishing
abdobooks.com

Jessica Rusick

ABDOBOOKS.COM

Published by Abdo Publishing, a division of ABDO, PO Box 398166, Minneapolis, Minnesota 55439.

Printed in the United States of America, North Mankato, Minnesota.

102020

012021

Design: Kelly Doudna, Mighty Media, Inc.

Production: Mighty Media, Inc.

Editor: Liz Salzmann

Cover Photographs: Shutterstock Images

Interior Photographs: AP Images, p. 34; Bob Houlihan/Flickr, pp. 38, 39; Carol M. Highsmith/ Library of Congress, pp. 4, 5; Carolina K. Smith/Shutterstock Images, pp. 28, 29; Chao Soi Cheong/AP Images, pp. 14, 15; Chris Hondros/AP Images, p. 37; Dave Martin/AP Images, pp. 32, 33; David Karp/AP Images, pp. 19, 44; David Lloyd/AP Images, p. 12; Eric Draper/Flickr, pp. 20, 21, 31, 45; Gulnara Samoilova/AP Images, p. 16; Hillery Smith Garrison/AP Images, p. 35; Pete Souza/Wikimedia Commons, p. 41; Photo courtesy of the city of Marietta/Flickr, p. 18; Robert F. Bukaty/AP Images, p. 23; Sgt. 1st Class Jerry Saslav/Flickr, p. 7; Shutterstock Images, pp. 1 (both), 8, 10, 11, 24, 25, 27, 30, 42

Design Elements: Shutterstock Images

LIBRARY OF CONGRESS CONTROL NUMBER: 2020940248

PUBLISHER'S CATALOGING-IN-PUBLICATION DATA

Names: Rusick, Jessica, author.

Title: September 11, 2001: then and now / by Jessica Rusick

Other title: then and now

Description: Minneapolis, Minnesota : Abdo Publishing, 2021 | Series: The 9/11 terrorist attacks | Includes online resources and index

Identifiers: ISBN 9781532194511 (lib. bdg.) | ISBN 9781098213879 (ebook)

Subjects: LCSH: September 11 Terrorist Attacks, 2001--Juvenile literature. | Acts of terrorism--Juvenile literature. | Terrorism--New York (State)--Juvenile literature. | Patriot Day--Juvenile literature. | United States--History--Juvenile literature.

Classification: DDC 973.931--dc23

TABLE OF CONTENTS

A Nation Under Attack 5

The Twin Towers Fall 15

Leaders Take Action 21

Ground Zero 25

Preventing Terrorism 29

The War on Terror 33

The Next Twenty Years 39

Timeline 44

Glossary 46

Online Resources 47

Index 48

The WTC's Twin Towers before the 9/11 terrorist attacks

Chapter 1

A NATION UNDER ATTACK

On September 11, 2001, the United States faced an emergency like no other. It began when terrorists boarded four airplanes as passengers and then hijacked the planes mid-flight. The terrorists flew two of the planes into the Twin Towers of the World Trade Center (WTC) complex in New York City. Both towers collapsed.

The terrorists on the third plane flew it into the Pentagon in Washington, DC. The fourth plane crashed in a field in Pennsylvania after the passengers and crew fought to regain control of the plane.

Together, these four incidents are known as the 9/11 terrorist attacks. Nearly 3,000 people were killed. This included all passengers and crew on the airplanes, people in and near the buildings the aircraft crashed into, and rescue workers who sought to help victims. The 9/11 terrorist attacks were the deadliest to occur on

US soil. People all over the world were shocked by the violent and tragic events of September 11.

Flight 11

At 7:59 a.m. on September 11, American Airlines Flight 11 took off from Boston, Massachusetts. It was headed for Los Angeles, California. The trip was routine for flight attendants Betty Ong and Madeline Sweeney. Not long after takeoff, however, the unthinkable happened.

At 8:19 a.m., Ong used one of the plane's phones to call airline ground staff. She told them that the plane had been hijacked. Five passengers had risen from their seats and stabbed another passenger and two crew members. Then, these hijackers took over flying the plane. Over the next 25 minutes, Ong calmly communicated what was happening on Flight 11. She also shared the assigned seat numbers of at least two of the hijackers. This helped officials identify the men through the plane's ticket records.

At 8:32 a.m., Sweeney also called airport ground staff. She reported additional details about the hijacking, including that one hijacker had shown her a bomb. She also gave physical descriptions of the hijackers.

As Ong and Sweeney talked, the plane tilted suddenly, flying lower and lower over New York City. At 8:45 a.m., Sweeney said, "I see the water. I see the buildings. I see buildings. . . . Oh, my God."

"Pray for us," Ong repeated several times. Then the calls abruptly ended.

PIVOTAL PEOPLE: ONG AND SWEENEY

Betty Ann Ong grew up in San Francisco's Chinatown neighborhood. As an adult, Ong enjoyed working with children and playing team sports. After her death, Ong's family created the Betty Ann Ong Foundation. This charity helps educate children about exercise and healthy eating. In 2011, the Chinatown Recreation Center in San Francisco was renamed the Betty Ann Ong Chinese Recreation Center.

Madeline "Amy" Sweeney lived with her husband and two children in Acton, Massachusetts. Sweeney is remembered as being calm during the chaos and fear caused by the hijacking. Shortly after the attacks, the government of Massachusetts established the Madeline Amy Sweeney Award for Civilian Bravery. This award is given to Massachusetts citizens who risk their lives to help others.

In 2014, Michael DeSousa (*second from left*) received the Madeline Amy Sweeney Award for Civilian Bravery for helping people escape a burning building.

Flight 11 Strikes the North Tower

In New York City, the morning of September 11, 2001, was sunny and clear. Downtown bustled. By 8:30 a.m., about 17,000 people had arrived at work at the WTC. This 16-acre (6.5 ha) complex's seven buildings held a hotel and various offices. There was a large shopping mall under the complex. The two tallest buildings

Smoke billows out of the North Tower where Flight 11 crashed into it.

were 1 WTC and 2 WTC, also called the North and South Towers. Together, the two buildings were known as the Twin Towers.

Constance Labetti worked in an office on the ninety-ninth floor of the South Tower. At 8:46 a.m., she looked out the window and froze. An airplane was flying past the building. It was so close that she could see into the plane's cockpit. Labetti watched in horror as Flight 11 crashed into floors 93 through 99 of the North Tower.

Everyone on the plane and many people in the North Tower died from the impact. And people throughout the building felt it shake, as if there had been an earthquake. The plane's tens of thousands of gallons of jet fuel ignited into a massive fireball. Smoke and fire began to fill the offices and corridors of the floors closest to where the plane crashed.

Evacuations Begin

People on the ground stared at the scene in awe. Many called emergency services. Within minutes, firefighters, police officers, and paramedics rushed to the building to begin evacuating survivors.

News teams also rushed to the scene and aired live video of the smoking tower. Civilians, first responders, and reporters alike struggled to understand what was happening. At first, most people assumed the crash had been an accident.

People in the North Tower immediately began evacuating. At 9:00 a.m., officials ordered people to evacuate neighboring buildings as well. In the towers, people crowded into the stairwells to escape. However, they moved in a calm and orderly fashion in spite of the panic. Many people helped others who were injured. The lines down the stairs often moved slowly, but there was little pushing, shoving, or line cutting.

The burning Twin Towers could be seen from miles away.

Flight 175

United Airlines Flight 175 took off about fifteen minutes after American Airlines Flight 11. The aircraft was scheduled to fly from Boston to Los Angeles that morning. But it was also taken over by five hijackers who turned the plane toward New York City.

At 9:03 a.m., as evacuations were in progress at the WTC, Flight 175 struck floors 77 through 85 of the South Tower. News programs broadcast the shocking live images to millions of people watching around the country. As flames and smoke shot out of the South Tower, it became clear that the first crash had not been an accident. The United States was under attack.

The Pentagon

As soon as Flight 175 hit the WTC, top officials at the National Military Command Center (NMCC) within the Pentagon started gathering information and preparing to respond. As Pentagon officials worked, American Airlines Flight 77 flew low over Washington, DC. At 9:37 a.m., the plane slammed into the first floor of the Pentagon. Everyone aboard the plane and 125 people inside the Pentagon were killed instantly.

Survivors crawled through burning, smoke-filled corridors to escape. As the building evacuated, some workers went back inside to look for more survivors. As dangerous smoke spread through the building, top officials moved to a secret location. Engineers stayed in the NMCC to keep its computer systems working. Their work ensured that the US military could keep responding to the attacks.

Unlike the WTC, the Pentagon was not completely destroyed in the attack.

Flight 93

The Federal Aviation Administration (FAA) regulates US air traffic. At 9:42 a.m., it grounded all civilian flights in hopes of preventing further attacks. But the order came too late for United Airlines Flight 93. It had taken off from Newark Liberty International Airport in New Jersey an hour earlier.

At 9:28, hijackers broke into the cockpit and took control of the flight. Passengers gathered in the back of the plane, talking to officials and family members on the plane's phones. In these

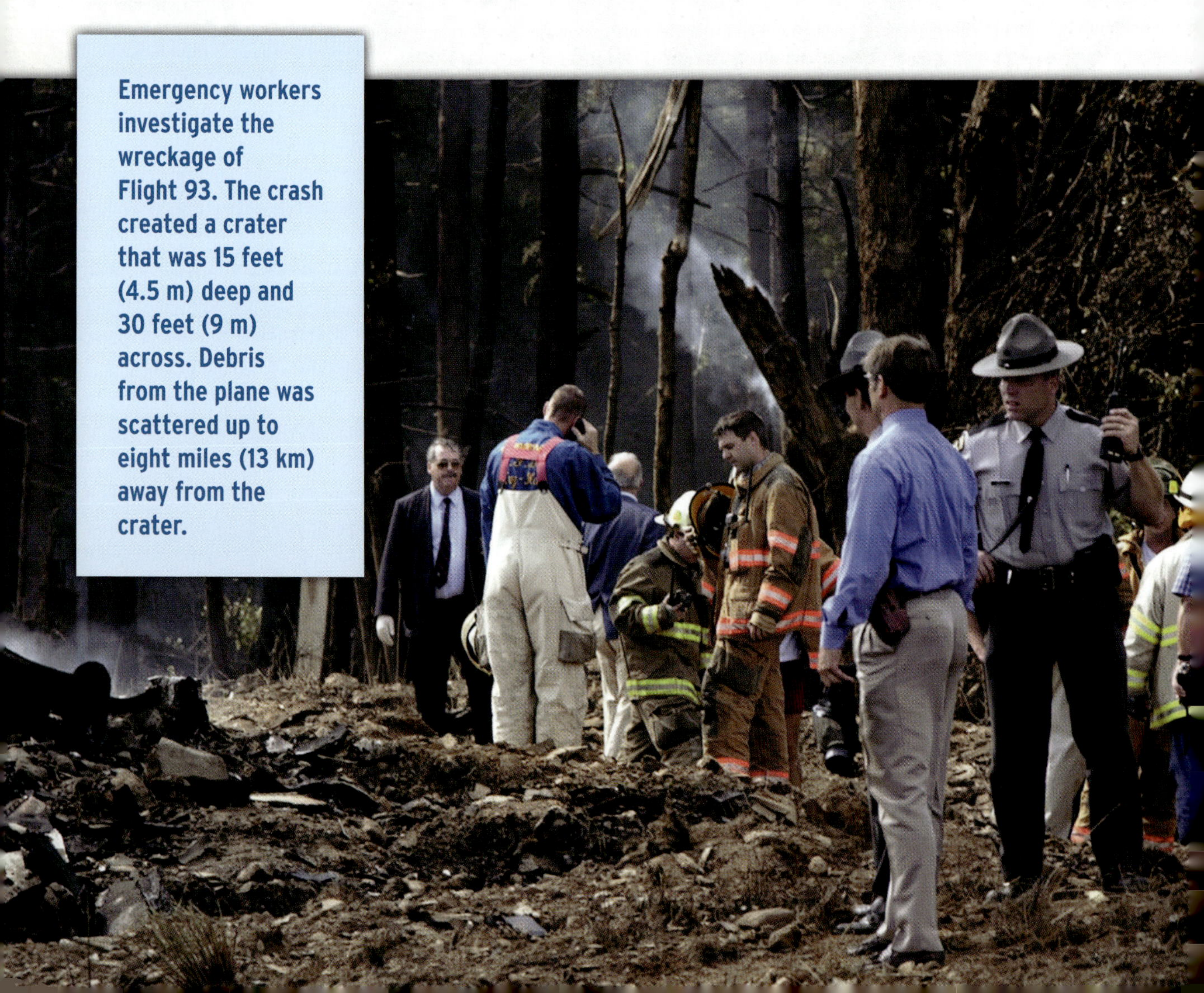

Emergency workers investigate the wreckage of Flight 93. The crash created a crater that was 15 feet (4.5 m) deep and 30 feet (9 m) across. Debris from the plane was scattered up to eight miles (13 km) away from the crater.

conversations, they learned about the WTC and Pentagon attacks. The group soon realized that Flight 93 was part of a larger attack.

Some of the passengers decided to storm the plane's cockpit to stop the hijackers. During the struggle, the hijackers decided to crash the plane rather than let the passengers get control of it. At 10:03 a.m., Flight 93 crashed into a Pennsylvania field at nearly 600 miles per hour (966 kmh). Everyone on board was killed.

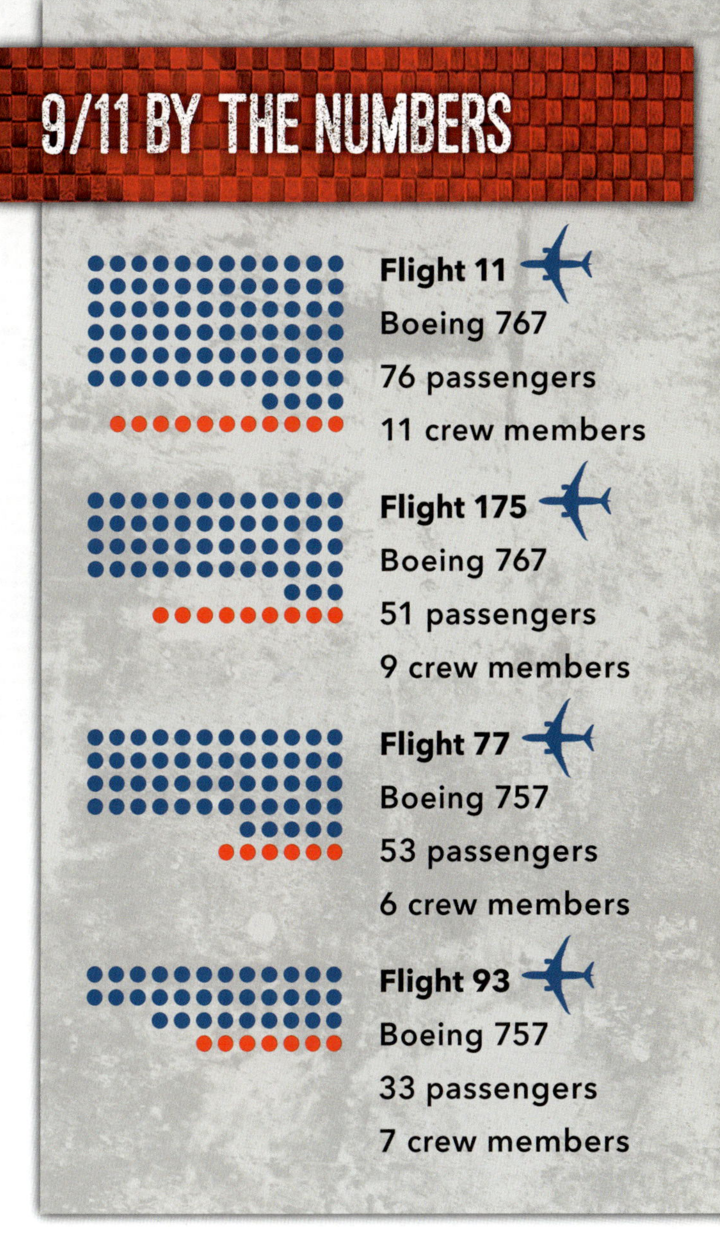

Evidence recovered from the crash suggested that the plane had been flying toward Washington, DC. Many believe that had the passengers not acted, Flight 93 could have crashed into the US Capitol Building or the White House.

An explosion after the plane hit the South Tower caused metal and glass to rain down on the streets below. Falling debris and bodies killed and injured people on the ground.

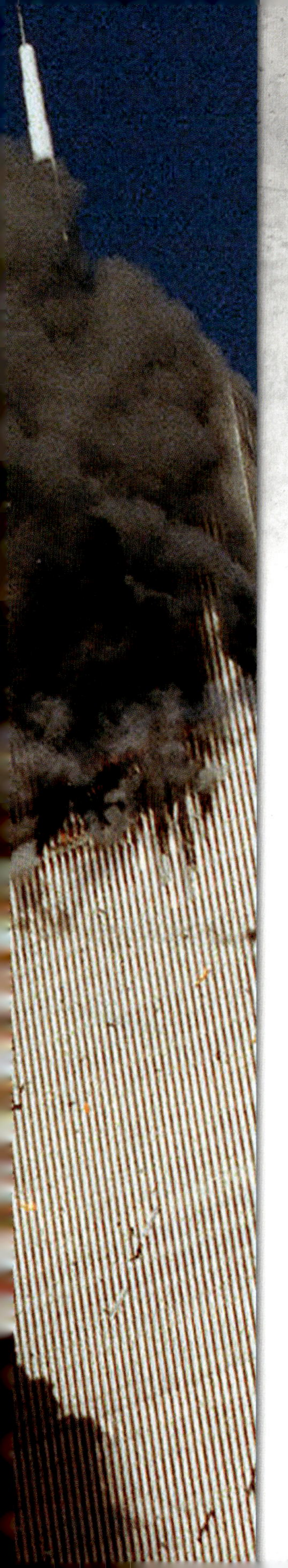

Chapter 2

THE TWIN TOWERS FALL

As Flight 93 crashed in Pennsylvania, evacuation of the Twin Towers was still underway. The White House and Capitol in Washington, DC, had also been evacuated, as had tall buildings in other cities around the country. National officials feared another attack could happen at any minute.

Meanwhile, fires raged inside the WTC. Firefighters quickly realized they couldn't put out the fires on the upper floors. So, they focused on saving as many people as possible. As office workers moved in lines down stairwells, firefighters ran upstairs to search for more survivors. Outside the buildings, police and paramedics guided survivors away from the towers to waiting ambulances.

In both towers, the planes had destroyed stairwells on the floors where they hit. Hundreds of people on floors above the crashes were trapped in the burning towers. To escape the flames, some people jumped out of windows to their deaths.

The South Tower

As paramedics continued to treat survivors, a loud cracking sound came from the South Tower. At 9:59 a.m., the building buckled near the crash site. The top of the tower tilted to one side. Within ten seconds, the entire building collapsed.

On the ground, a wave of pressure threw people from their feet. Others ran as a massive cloud of dust and debris swallowed nearby streets. The force of the tower falling damaged many nearby buildings.

The top of the South Tower leans to the side as the building begins to collapse.

The North Tower

After the South Tower fell, fire department commanders ordered firefighters to leave the North Tower. However, their radio signals were not strong enough to reach firefighters on higher floors. So, many firefighters did not hear the orders to evacuate. Less than half an hour later, at 10:28 a.m., the North Tower fell, its 110 stories crashing down on one another.

Reasons for the Collapse

The impact of the planes seemed to directly affect fewer than ten floors of each tower. So, many people wondered how this could lead to the entire buildings collapsing. There are two main reasons the towers collapsed.

First, the impact of the airplanes destroyed many of buildings' outer support columns, which put extra pressure on the remaining columns. In addition, the intense heat from the jet fuel fires likely weakened the building's internal steel supports. Heat from the fire spread from metal beam to metal beam. Eventually, many of the supporting beams throughout the towers were affected.

The Aftermath

Survivors of the WTC attacks wandered the streets, covered in dust and blood. Some went home. Others found pay phones or cell phones to call their loved ones.

Many who were injured made their way to hospitals. Hospitals near the WTC had prepared medical staff to help survivors. After

PIVOTAL PEOPLE: JOSEPHINE HARRIS AND THE LADDER 6 FIREFIGHTERS

Few people who were still inside the towers when they collapsed survived. But office worker Josephine Harris and the firefighters of Ladder 6 defied the odds. While evacuating the North Tower, the six firefighters met Harris. She had made it partway down the stairs, but a previous leg injury had left her exhausted. The firefighters knew helping Harris would slow them down. But they refused to leave her behind. The firefighters and Harris were still in the stairwell when the North Tower collapsed on top of them. Yet, everyone in the group survived!

The Ladder 6 firefighters were led by Captain Jay Jonas (*left*).

A wall in New York City displays posters of people missing after the 9/11 terrorist attacks.

the towers collapsed, hundreds of patients came in with severe burns or cuts from glass. Others couldn't breathe after inhaling the dust in the air.

Within hours of the attacks, missing person posters appeared throughout New York City. Families hoped their missing loved ones might still be found. Many of these signs remained in place around the city for months.

President Bush (*left*) visited the WTC site on September 14, 2001. He gave a speech to encourage and thank firefighters and rescue workers.

Chapter 3

LEADERS TAKE ACTION

Leaders responded quickly to the 9/11 terrorist attacks. President George W. Bush was visiting an elementary school in Florida that day, reading books to children. White House Chief of Staff Andrew Card, who was at the school with Bush, was told of the attacks. He then whispered the news to the president.

From an empty classroom, Bush called other leaders, including Vice President Dick Cheney and New York governor George E. Pataki. Bush was then flown to a secure Air Force base in Louisiana, where he continued to respond to the attacks.

America's Mayor

New York City mayor Rudolph "Rudy" Giuliani began communicating with fire chiefs after the towers were hit. He was two blocks from the towers when they fell. In the aftermath, Giuliani worked to send food and lights to those cleaning up the wreckage. He also told residents to evacuate the neighborhood around the WTC. Hours later, Giuliani gave updates to the public at a press conference.

Giuliani would give many more updates to New Yorkers and the American people before his term ended on January 1, 2002. Many Americans praised Giuliani's calm and capable leadership after the attacks. Due to this, he was sometimes called "America's Mayor."

Reassuring the People

The night of the attacks, President Bush addressed the nation from the White House. He said, "Terrorist attacks can shake the foundations of our biggest buildings, but they cannot touch the foundation of America."

Bush also took action to protect the US from future terrorist attacks. Eight days after the 9/11 terrorist attacks, Bush announced the creation of the Office of Homeland Security (OHS). This new office combined several existing government agencies and services into one large agency. The main mission of the OHS was to "develop and coordinate the implementation of a comprehensive national strategy to secure the United States from terrorist threats or attacks."

Congress Gets Involved

Leaders in Congress wanted to help those who had been injured in the attacks and the families of those who died. To that end, Congress passed the Air Transportation Safety and System Stabilization Act. President Bush signed it on September 22, 2001.

This act included the September 11th Victim Compensation Fund (VCF). The fund provided money for people and families affected by the 9/11 terrorist attacks as well as the cleanup and recovery efforts. With the leadership of Congress, President Bush, Governor Pataki, and Mayor Giuliani, the United States began the long process of healing from the attacks.

The day after the 9/11 terrorist attacks, Giuliani (*center*) visited the WTC site with Pataki (*left*) and New York senator Hillary Clinton (*right*).

With eight floors, 6 WTC was the shortest building in the complex. It was severely damaged by the collapse of the Twin Towers. The remaining parts of the building were torn down during the Ground Zero cleanup.

Chapter 4

GROUND ZERO

Rescue and cleanup efforts at the WTC began immediately. In the days after the attack, people began referring to the site as Ground Zero. Firefighters, rescue workers, and police officers cleared away rubble at Ground Zero. Because the wreckage was unstable and likely to collapse further, debris had to be removed carefully, bucket by bucket.

Cleanup Begins

Only 20 people were recovered alive from the wreckage. A search-and-rescue dog discovered the last survivor 27 hours after the attack. Ten days after the attacks, the hope of finding survivors had faded. Instead, efforts turned to recovering human remains and artifacts.

In the days after the attacks, the Environmental Protection Agency said the air around Ground Zero was safe to breathe, although they recommended that those working at Ground Zero wear protective masks or respirators.

However, masks were not enforced, so many workers did not wear them. The air was actually filled with particles of metal, cement dust, asbestos, and other dangerous substances. Many people exposed to this air later became sick with respiratory diseases and cancer.

As cleanup work continued, all seven buildings in the WTC complex had collapsed or had to be destroyed. As the wreckage became more stable, debris could be hauled away in large trucks.

9/11 BY THE NUMBERS

Between September 11 and October 30, 2001, the American Red Cross received nearly 1.2 million units of blood. That is about three times more units than they would normally collect during this period. A unit is about one pint (450 mL) of blood.

Coming Together

Many Americans helped survivors and those working at the attack sites during this scary time. In New York City, volunteers served food and delivered water to those working at Ground Zero. Cities across the nation sent firefighters to work at Ground Zero. Around the country, many people donated blood. They wanted to do something to help those injured in the attacks.

The world showed its support as well. People from 78 countries died in the attacks. Some were on the hijacked planes. Others were

Alicia Keys was one of 21 performers at the "America: A Tribute to Heroes" concert. The event aired on all four major TV networks on September 21, 2001.

visiting or working at the crash sites. On September 12, French newspaper *Le Monde* ran the headline, "Today, we are all Americans." The next day in the United Kingdom, Queen Elizabeth II instructed the guards at Buckingham Palace to play the US national anthem.

Helping Survivors

Two benefit concerts, "America: A Tribute to Heroes" and "The Concert for New York City," were held in the fall of 2001. The concerts honored victims and first responders and raised money for survivors and victims' families. These concerts and other charities raised $2.8 billion to help those affected by the attacks.

Government leaders also worked to help those who needed support. On December 21, 2001, Congress created the VCF. This fund gave money to people injured in the attacks and to the families of those killed.

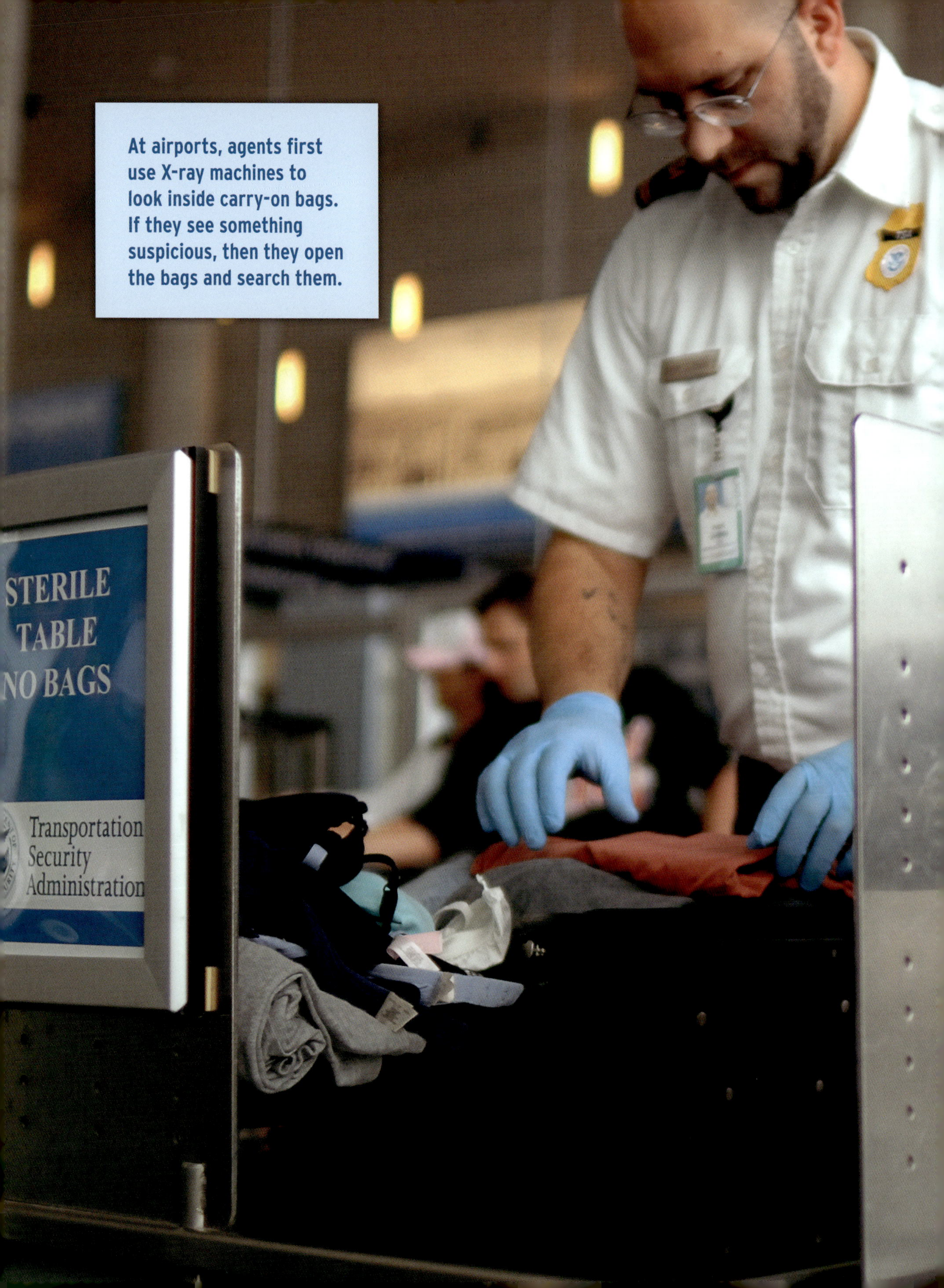

At airports, agents first use X-ray machines to look inside carry-on bags. If they see something suspicious, then they open the bags and search them.

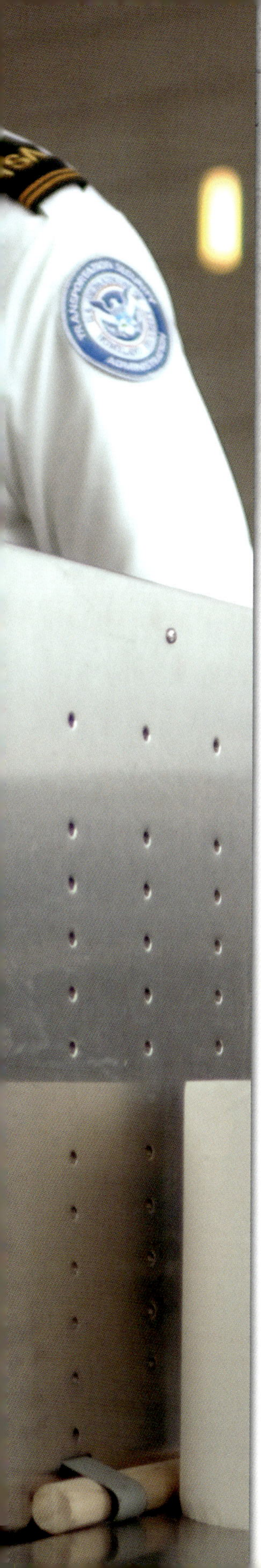

Chapter 5

PREVENTING TERRORISM

In addition to supporting survivors of the attacks, there was a need to protect the country from possible future terrorist attacks. Immediately following the 9/11 terrorist attacks, all civilian flights were cancelled until September 13. When airports reopened, many did so with new security measures.

One of these measures further limited the items that passengers could bring onto airplanes in carry-on bags. At the time of the 9/11 terrorist attacks, guns and large knives were already banned from flights, but passengers could bring small blades onboard. These included scissors, pocketknives, and box cutters.

It is believed that the 9/11 terrorists used box cutters as weapons during the hijackings. Because of this, passengers were no longer allowed to bring sharp tools of any type or size in their carry-on bags. However, passengers could still pack small blades in checked luggage that was loaded into the cargo hold.

2001 VS. TODAY

Airport security was very different before 9/11. Airlines weren't as strict about requiring passengers to show a form of identification, or ID. And anyone could enter an airport and visit its gates to see travelers off or meet incoming passengers. Also, only carry-on bags were scanned to check for dangerous items. Checked bags often weren't. Today, everyone has to show ID when buying tickets and going through security. Only people with plane tickets can go past security to the gates. And all carry-on and checked luggage is screened before it is allowed on a plane.

The USA PATRIOT Act

After 9/11, Congress worked to prevent future attacks. In October 2001, it passed the USA PATRIOT Act. This act made it easier for federal agents to search citizens' phone and computer records. The agents could then use these records to investigate communications that could be related to future acts of terrorism. The act had wide political support when it passed. However, in later

Increased security measures often led to long lines at airport security checkpoints.

years, some politicians and human rights groups felt the act violated people's privacy. In 2015, President Barack Obama changed the USA PATRIOT Act to limit the data federal agencies could collect.

Airport Security

Congress was also concerned about airport security after 9/11. In November 2001, it passed the Aviation and Transportation Security Act. Before 9/11, each airport and airline had its own security rules. The act standardized the rules and implemented strict new ones. The act also established the Transportation Security Administration (TSA). The TSA is the organization that supervises and enforces security in all US airports.

Bush (*seated*) signed the USA PATRIOT Act on October 26, 2001.

Some of the attacks in the war on terror were launched from the aircraft carrier USS *Carl Vinson*.

Chapter 6

THE WAR ON TERROR

As the American public tried to make sense of the attacks, the country's leaders pieced together who was behind them. It took months to learn the full details of the plot. However, within days, investigators determined that 19 members of the terrorist group al-Qaeda were responsible. These terrorists had spent years planning the attacks. This included training in US flight schools.

Al-Qaeda is an Islamist terrorist group. Its members believe that Middle Eastern countries should enforce strict laws based on Islam. Al-Qaeda members believe in using violence to achieve this goal.

People who follow Islam are called Muslims. Most Muslims do not agree with al-Qaeda's views. In fact, many Muslims think al-Qaeda's beliefs and actions go against the teachings of Islam.

The War in Afghanistan

Osama bin Laden was al-Qaeda's leader in 2001.

Osama bin Laden

Bin Laden lived in the Middle Eastern country of Afghanistan. There, a strict government called the Taliban supported al-Qaeda. Bin Laden hoped the 9/11 terrorist attacks would limit or stop US involvement in Middle Eastern affairs. That way, governments supported by al-Qaeda could rise to power.

On September 20, 2001, President Bush announced the war on terror to Congress and the world. The war began the next month in Afghanistan with Operation Enduring Freedom. US forces launched attacks on Taliban and al-Qaeda bases. By December, the US had overthrown the Taliban. Unfortunately, many al-Qaeda leaders, including bin Laden, escaped.

The US military then began helping the Afghan people rebuild Afghanistan's government. In November 2014, the US officially ended combat operations in Afghanistan. However, many troops remained to help the country rebuild.

The War in Iraq

One year after the 9/11 terrorist attacks, the United States learned of a possible terrorist threat in the Middle Eastern country of Iraq. At the time, Iraq was ruled by a dictator named Saddam Hussein. In 2002, the Bush administration told Congress that Hussein possessed weapons of mass destruction (WMDs). These included nuclear, chemical, and biological weapons.

Bush addressed the American people on October 7, 2001, to announce that the war with Afghanistan had begun.

RISE OF ANTI-MUSLIM DISCRIMINATION

Prior to the 9/11 terrorist attacks, Muslims had long faced prejudice in American society. For example, until 1944, Muslims were often denied US citizenship. After 9/11, prejudice against Muslims increased. Two days after the 9/11 terrorist attacks, several hundred people stormed a mosque in Chicago, Illinois, and refused to leave. On September 15, 2001, a Muslim store owner in Texas was murdered. Overall, the number of assaults on Muslims went up 800 percent between 2000 and 2001.

Bush and other leaders were concerned that the WMDs would be used in terrorist attacks. Bush wanted to remove Hussein from power and find these weapons. In October 2002, Congress voted to authorize going to war in Iraq. The war began in March 2003.

Success and Failure

By the end of 2003, one goal of the war was accomplished. In April, US troops captured Iraq's capital city, Baghdad. Saddam Hussein was arrested in December 2003 and executed by Iraqis in 2006. However, US troops did not find WMDs. This led some US lawmakers and citizens to believe the Bush administration had misled lawmakers by saying the weapons existed. Over time, the war became increasingly unpopular among Americans, including some who had initially supported it.

Ongoing Conflict

In May 2003, President Bush had announced the end of major combat operations in Iraq. However, the war lasted much longer. Many different groups in Iraq were fighting for power. So, US troops stayed in Iraq to help maintain order and establish a democratic government. The Iraq War officially ended on December 18, 2011. However, as in Afghanistan, some US soldiers stayed behind to continue the rebuilding effort.

Hussein was tried in a Baghdad court for crimes against humanity. The trial started in October 2005. He was found guilty on November 5, 2006, and hanged on December 30, 2006.

The final steel beam from the WTC was cut down on May 28, 2002. It was removed from the site during a ceremony two days later. Today, the beam is on display in the 9/11 Memorial Museum.

Chapter 7

THE NEXT TWENTY YEARS

Several months after the United States began its war on terror, cleanup efforts at the WTC were wrapping up. On May 30, 2002, a ceremony at Ground Zero marked the end of cleanup. The project had finished ahead of schedule. At the Pentagon, crews had worked long hours for five weeks to clean up the wreckage there. In August 2002, Pentagon employees began moving back into the repaired sections of the building.

Lasting Effects

Though the wreckage was cleared, the road to recovery was still long. Mental health became a concern. In the aftermath of the attacks, almost half of all Americans had symptoms of stress and depression. Some survivors and first responders also experienced post-traumatic stress disorder (PTSD). This made it difficult to sleep, deal with strong emotions, and go back to work. Although PTSD symptoms for many have declined over the years following the attacks, cases in rescue workers and firefighters have gone up since 2001.

An Ongoing Toll

The 9/11 terrorist attacks killed 2,977 people. This included 184 at the Pentagon, 40 in Pennsylvania, and 2,753 at the WTC. Although the death toll was staggering, it could have been far worse without orderly evacuations and the help of first responders. At the WTC, 87 percent of the 17,400 people in the Twin Towers were safely evacuated.

The 9/11 terrorist attacks continue to affect the survivors. Since 2001, more than 40,000 first responders and survivors have been diagnosed with illnesses caused by breathing the toxic dust at Ground Zero. The VCF was reactivated in 2011 and then renewed in 2015 to continue helping pay for their medical care. By 2019, more than 1,300 people had died from these illnesses.

9/11 BY THE NUMBERS

More than 3 million hours of labor were spent on Ground Zero cleanup. More than 100,000 truckloads of debris were removed from the site. Altogether, the debris weighed more than 1.8 million tons (1.6 million t)!

President Barack Obama (*second from left*) and members of the national security team receive reports during the operation to capture bin Laden.

The War Continues

The war on terror also took a toll. After nearly ten years of fighting in the Middle East, US Navy SEALs located and killed Osama bin Laden in Pakistan on May 1, 2011. Many Americans said that bin Laden's death made them feel safer. However, the conflicts in Afghanistan and Iraq continued after bin Laden's death. By 2020, thousands of American soldiers had died in Afghanistan and Iraq. Hundreds of thousands of Afghan and Iraqi soldiers and civilians had died as well. And the war on terror is still being fought.

Rebuilding and Rebirth

After Ground Zero was cleared, city officials, designers, and architects began working on plans to rebuild the WTC complex. On September 12, 2011, a memorial at the WTC opened to the public. It featured two large pools where the Twin Towers once stood.

The names of those killed in the attacks were inscribed near the pools.

In May 2014, the 9/11 Memorial Museum opened. It featured artifacts and wreckage from Ground Zero. It also included the stories of victims, survivors, and first responders.

One World Trade Center

In November 2014, One World Trade Center opened. Construction on this tower had begun in 2006. It was the centerpiece of the new WTC complex. Other buildings in the complex have also been completed.

9/11 BY THE NUMBERS

One World Trade Center is 1,776 feet (541 m) tall. This number represents the year the United States declared independence from Great Britain.

Pentagon Memorial

Memorials were also constructed near the other attack sites. A memorial to the Pentagon victims was dedicated on September 11, 2008.

It sits on a two-acre (0.8 ha) plot near the crash site. The memorial includes 184 benches, each representing a victim of the attack.

The Tower of Voices

In September 2018, the Tower of Voices memorial was completed to honor the victims of Flight 93. The monument is located at the crash site in Pennsylvania. The tower stands a symbolic 93 feet (28 m) high. It includes 40 wind chimes to honor the 40 passengers and crew members who lost their lives in 2001.

Remembering 9/11

The attacks on September 11, 2001, have been remembered in many ways over the years. Films have been made about the WTC attacks and the Flight 93 crash. Books, documentaries, and television specials tell the stories of victims and survivors in new ways.

Museums, apps, and interactive websites also help people learn about the 9/11 terrorist attacks. And, there are still ways to help or honor those affected by the attacks. Charities continue to serve first responders and the children of victims. In addition, September 11 has been declared a National Day of Service and Remembrance.

Twenty years later, the 9/11 terrorist attacks continue to impact and shape American society. Their effects can be felt in extra security precautions and increased surveillance. They can be felt in the lives of children who grew up without one or both of their parents. And, they can be felt in the memorials that pledge to never forget.

TIMELINE

SEPTEMBER 11, 2001

8:46 A.M.
American Airlines Flight 11 crashes into the North Tower of the WTC.

9:03 A.M.
United Airlines Flight 175 crashes into the South Tower of the WTC.

9:37 A.M.
American Airlines Flight 77 crashes into the Pentagon in Washington, DC.

9:42 A.M.
The FAA grounds all civilian flights in the United States.

9:59 A.M.
The South Tower collapses.

10:03 A.M.
United Airlines Flight 93 crashes in a Pennsylvania field.

10:28 A.M.
The North Tower collapses.

2003

MARCH 2003
The Iraq War begins.

2008

SEPTEMBER 11, 2008
A memorial honoring the victims of the Pentagon attack is dedicated.

2001

OCTOBER 2001
The war in Afghanistan begins.

NOVEMBER 2001
Congress passes the Aviation and Transportation Security Act.

2002

MAY 30, 2002
A ceremony marks the end of the Ground Zero cleanup.

AUGUST 2002
People begin moving back into the repaired portions of the Pentagon.

2011

MAY 1, 2011
US Navy SEALs kill Osama bin Laden in Pakistan.

SEPTEMBER 12, 2011
A 9/11 memorial at the WTC opens to the public.

DECEMBER 18, 2011
The Iraq War officially ends.

2014

MAY 2014
The 9/11 Memorial Museum opens.

NOVEMBER 2014
One World Trade Center opens. Combat operations in Afghanistan officially end.

2018

SEPTEMBER 2018
The Tower of Voices honoring the victims of Flight 93 is completed in Pennsylvania.

GLOSSARY

aftermath–the time immediately following a bad and usually destructive event.

architect–a person who plans and designs buildings.

artifact–an object remaining from a particular location or time period.

asbestos–minerals that builders once used to fireproof buildings. Today, scientists know that breathing in asbestos fibers can cause diseases such as cancer.

civilian–of or relating to something nonmilitary. A civilian is a person who is not an active member of the military.

democratic–related to a governmental system in which people vote on how to run their country.

diagnose–to recognize something, such as a disease, by signs, symptoms, or tests.

dictator–a ruler with complete control who often governs in a cruel way.

documentary–a film or television series that artistically presents facts, often about an event or a person.

hijack–to take over by threatening violence.

Iraq War–a conflict that began in March 2003 when the United States and its allies invaded Iraq. After the fall of the Iraqi government, US troops remained in Iraq to help stabilize the new government.

Islam–the religion of Muslims as described in the Koran. Islam is based on the teachings of the god Allah through the prophet Muhammad.

memorial–something that serves to remind people of a person or an event.

Muslim–a person who follows Islam.

paramedic–someone trained to care for a patient before or during the trip to a hospital.

Pentagon–the five-sided building near Washington, DC, where the main offices of the US Department of Defense are located.

post-traumatic stress disorder (PTSD)–a mental condition that can be caused by a very shocking or difficult experience. Symptoms of PTSD include depression and anxiety.

surveillance–close watch kept over someone or something.

violate–to take away or interfere with something in an unfair or illegal way.

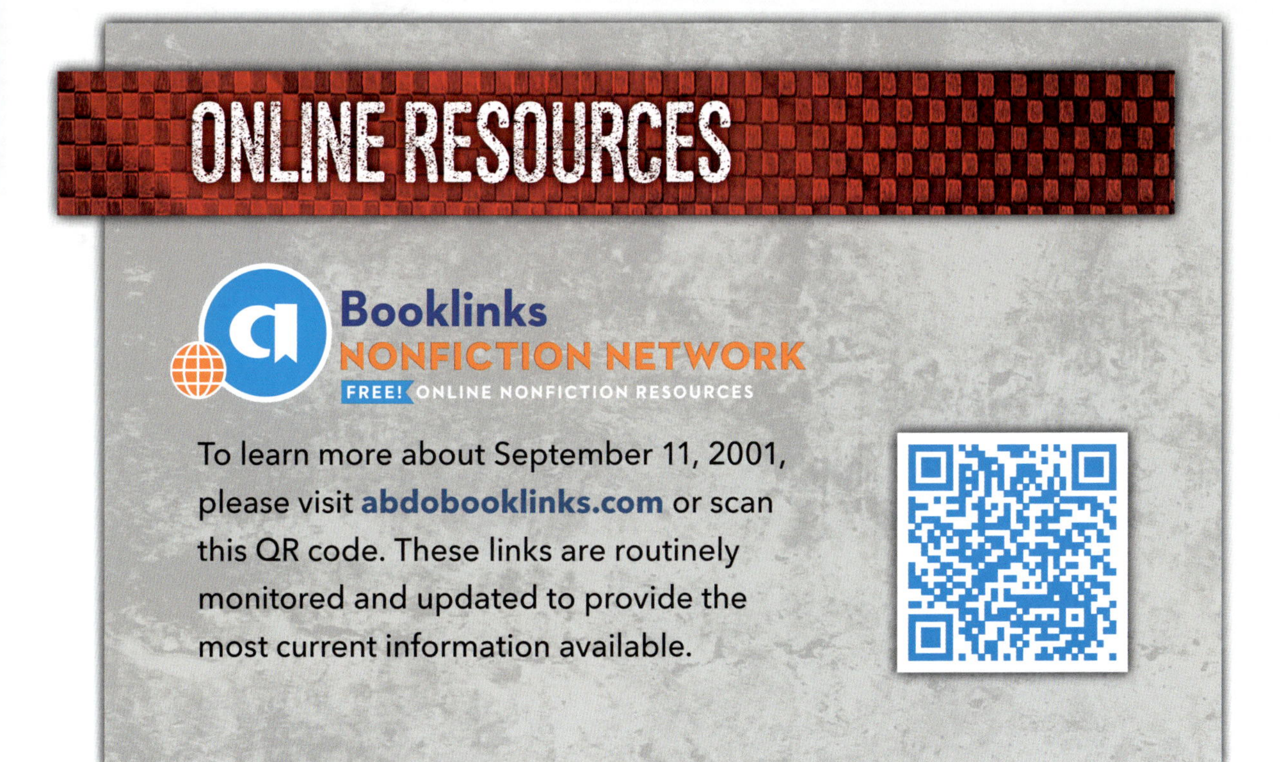

INDEX

A

Afghanistan, 33-34, 37, 41
Air Transportation Safety and System Stabilization Act, 22-23
airplanes, 5-6, 8-13, 15, 17, 29, 43
airport security, 29-31, 43
al-Qaeda, 33-34
Aviation and Transportation Security Act, 31

B

Baghdad, 36
benefit concerts, 27
bin Laden, Osama, 33-34, 41
Boston, Massachusetts, 6, 10
Buckingham Palace, 27
Bush, George W., 21-23, 35-37

C

Capitol Building, US, 13, 15
Card, Andrew, 21
Cheney, Dick, 21
Congress, US, 22-23, 27, 30-31, 35-36

D

Department of Defense, US, 11

E

Elizabeth II (queen), 27
Environmental Protection Agency, 25
evacuations, 9-11, 15, 18, 21-22, 40

F

Federal Aviation Administration (FAA), 12
firefighters, 9, 15, 17-18, 25-26, 40
first responders, 9, 27, 39-40, 42-43

G

Giuliani, Rudolph "Rudy," 21-23
Ground Zero, 25-26, 39-42

H

Harris, Josephine, 18
hijackers, 5-6, 10, 12-13, 29
hospitals, 17, 19
Hussein, Saddam, 35-36

I

Iraq, 35-37, 41
Islam, 33

L

Labetti, Constance, 9
Ladder 6, 18
Le Monde, 27

N

National Military Command Center (NMCC), 11
Navy SEALs, 41
New York City, 5-6, 8, 10, 19, 21-22, 26-27
9/11 Memorial & Museum, 41-42
9/11-related illnesses, 26, 39-40
North Tower, 8-9, 17-18

O

Obama, Barack, 31
Office of Homeland Security (OHS), 22
Ong, Betty Ann, 6-7
Operation Enduring Freedom, 34

P

Pakistan, 41
paramedics, 9, 15-16
Pataki, George E., 21, 23
Pennsylvania, 5, 13, 15, 40, 43
Pentagon, 5, 11-12, 39-40, 42-43
police officers, 9, 15, 25

R

rescue workers, 5, 25, 40

S

September 11th Victim Compensation Fund (VCF), 23, 27, 40
South Tower, 9-10, 16-17
survivors, 9, 11, 15-19, 25-27, 29, 39-40, 42-43
Sweeney, Madeline "Amy," 6-7

T

Taliban, 34
Tower of Voices, 43
Transportation Security Administration (TSA), 31
Twin Towers, 5, 9, 15, 40-41

U

USA PATRIOT Act, 30-31

W

war on terror, 33, 39, 41
Washington, DC, 5, 11, 13, 15
weapons of mass destruction (WMDs), 35-36
White House, 13, 15, 21-22
World Trade Center (WTC), 5, 8-11, 15, 17, 22, 25-26, 39-43